Doctor

ILLUSTRATED BY JESS STOCKHAM

You're the next patient on my list. Come in!

Are we going to see the doctor or the nurse?

What time is our appointment? Are we next?

We have to wait until it's our turn.

This shouldn't hurt. It will be very quick.

You can look the other way if you want to.

All done! That was your last injection.

Which sticker would you like? Can Baby have one too?

Let's measure your height. Stand up straight!

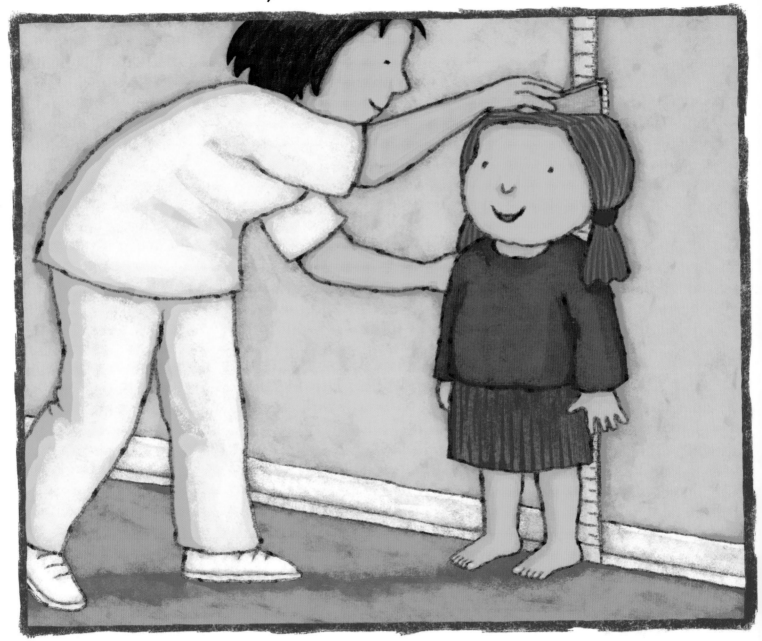

Like this? Am I taller now that I'm four?

The scales measure how heavy you are.

I'll make a note of your weight on my special chart.

I feel really hot and tired. Do you have a headache?

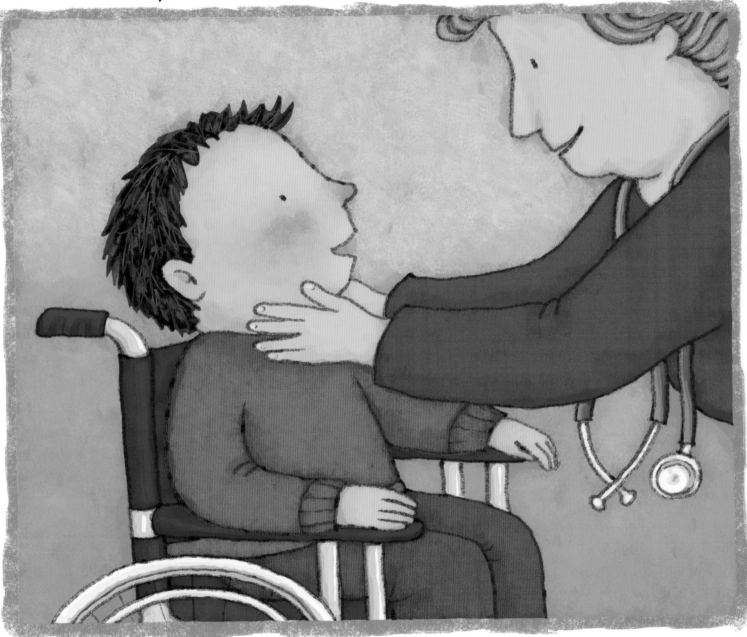

Let me feel if your glands are swollen.

I'll check your temperature with this thermometer.

It won't hurt. You'll just hear it go 'beep'.

My throat feels sore and I keep coughing.

I'll just listen with my stethoscope. It might feel cold!

Say 'Aah!' Now I can see the back of your throat.

You should get better without any medicine.

Oh dear, look at those spots on your tummy!

I think it looks like a heat rash.

If it hasn't gone in a few days, come back again.

It's important to ask the doctor if you're not sure.

I was doing a big jump and I fell off my board!

Does it hurt when I move it? What else hurts?

It's only a strain. This sling will support your arm.

Now go home and rest. It should feel better soon.

My ear is hurting. I can't hear properly. It feels hot.

I'll use this to look inside your ear. It looks swollen.

Take this prescription to the pharmacist.

We'll collect your medicine on the way home.

She's been feeling sick and isn't eating anything.

Lie still. The doctor will examine your tummy.

Does it hurt when I press here? Or here?

Make sure you rest and have lots to drink.

Your skin looks very sore and dry. I think it's eczema.

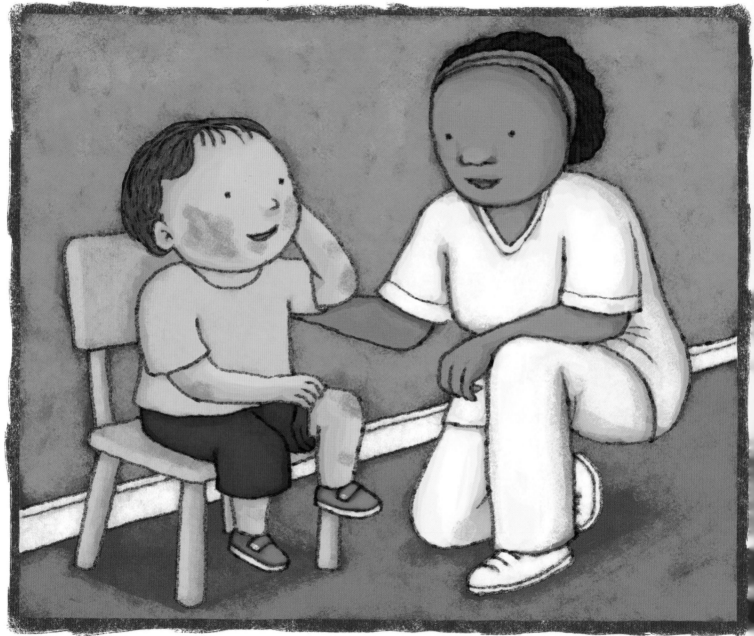

It's so itchy, I want to scratch it. Try not to.

It'll probably go away as you get older.

This cream will feel cool. It's very soothing.

Blow as hard as you can into the peak flow meter.

It measures how strong your lungs are.

This inhaler will help you breathe better with your asthma.

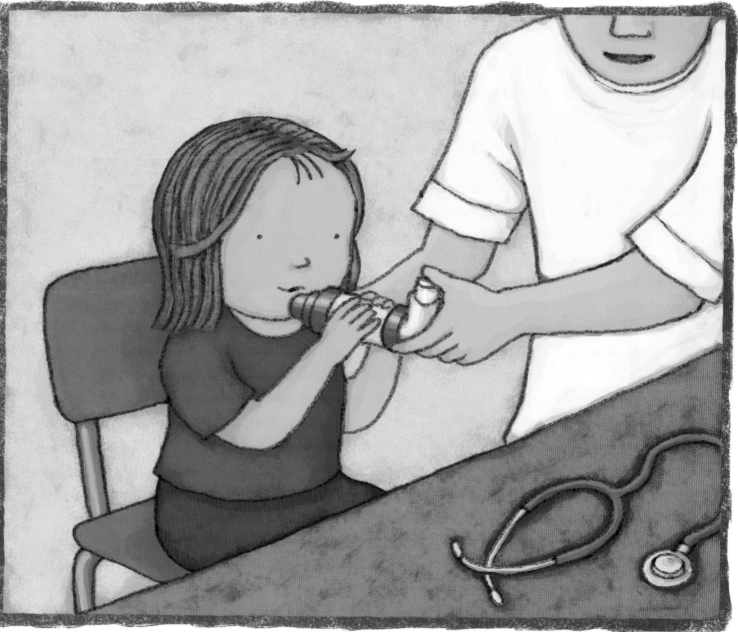

It puts the medicine straight into your lungs.

One spoonful of medicine now, and one later!

When can I go out and play with my friends?